a minedition book

published by Penguin Young Readers Group

Text copyright © 2005 by Brigitte Weninger
Illustrations copyright © 2005 by Eve Tharlet
Original title: Gemeinsam sind wir stark
English text translation by Kathryn Bishop
Coproduction with Michael Neugebauer Publishing Ltd., Hong Kong.
Rights arranged with "minedition" Rights and Licensing AG, Zurich, Switzerland.

Published simultaneously in Canada.
Manufactured in Hong Kong
by Wide World Ltd.
Typesetting in Icone
Color separation by
Fotoreproduzioni
Grafiche, Italy.

Library of Congress Cataloging-in-Publication Data available upon request.
ISBN 0-698-40034-8
10 9 8 7 6 5 4 3 2 1
First Impression

For more information please visit our website: www.minedition.com

One For All
-All For One

Brigitte Weninger

Illustrated by Eve Tharlet

Translated by Kathryn Bishop

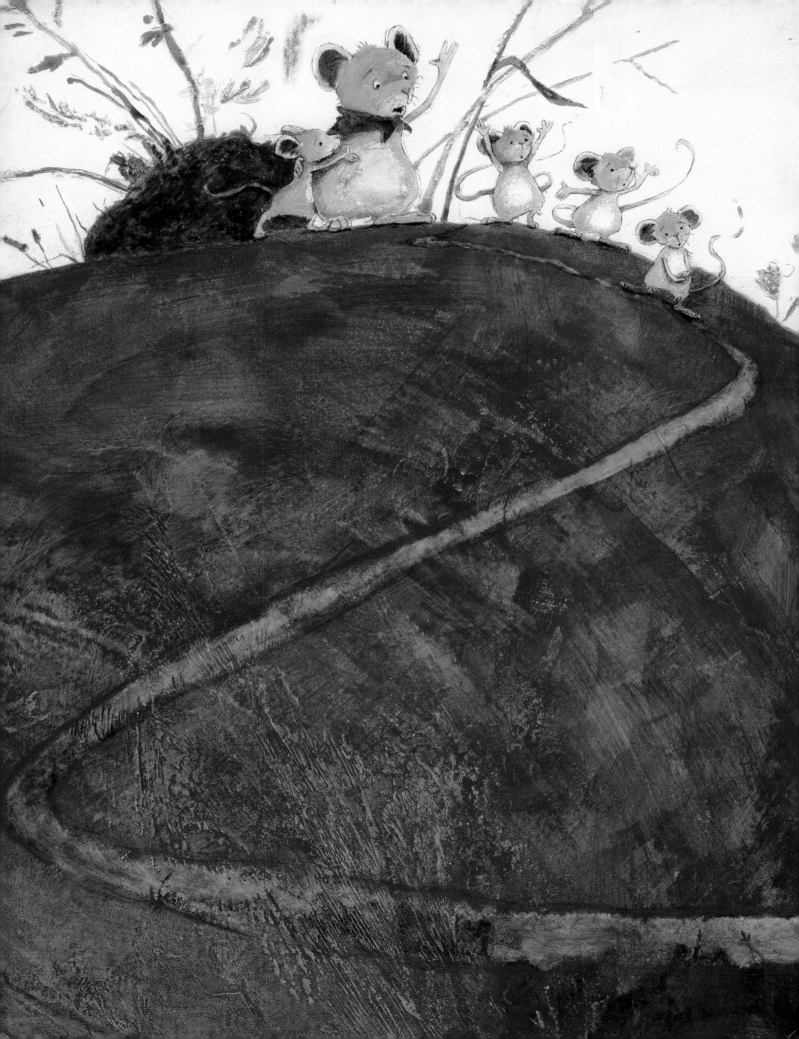

"Good-bye," said Max and hugged his family.
"We're going to miss you soooo much," cried
his brothers and sisters.
"I'll come back, I promise," said Max. "But
I'm big enough now to go out in the world.
I want to discover something new."
Mama Mouse nodded and said, "Follow your
dreams, Max, and never forget that you are
something special. Do this, and you will
also find good and special friends."

Max traveled cheerfully out into the world.
Once in a while he would stumble and fall, but that didn't bother him.
"That can happen when you try something new," Max said to himself.
"But I won't stay down because I have things to discover."

Just as Max was wriggling himself up, something hit him on the head.
"Ouch!" said Max. "What was that?"
"Oh, I... I'm sorry, that was my cane, I... I didn't see you," stuttered a
  little mole.
"Nonsense," said Max. "I'm certainly big enough, are you blind?"
"Not completely," said the little girl mole. "I just don't see very well.
  But I have a great nose for smelling things; even underground I can
  tell what's what."

"Then you're something special too!" said Max happily. "Just like me. One of my legs is too long and my whiskers are too short, so I fall down a lot. I am a very good thinker, though. Do you want to be friends and go out into the world together?"

"Oh, that would be wonderful," said Molly Mole. "Where will we be going?"
"To the place where dreams grow," said Max.
When they reached the edge of the pond Molly stopped.
"What's that jumping?" she asked.

"Oh, it's only a frog," said Max. "He's having fun. Wow, that was a somersault. Bravo, frog. That was great!"

The frog was surprised and said, "Ribbit... What?... Ribbit, ribbit?"

"Perhaps he didn't understand you. Frogs don't hear very well," said Molly.

"He may not hear very well," said Max, "but he can jump and laugh like a champion. He's something special just like us."

He put his arm out and touched the frog
gently and then said loudly, "Molly and
I are going out into the world together to
follow our dreams. Would you like to
come with us and be our friend?"
"Ribbit, Ribbit, yes,"
answered Freddy Frog happily.

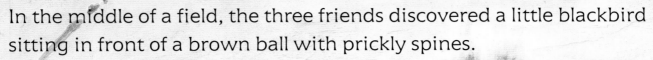

In the middle of a field, the three friends discovered a little blackbird sitting in front of a brown ball with prickly spines.

The little blackbird twittered, "Oh, please come out, please. I want to play with you."

And a little voice peeped back, "I don't think I can."

"Oh, please," said the bird.

"No, I'm afraid," said the little voice.

"Who are you talking to?" asked Max.

"It's Henry, he's a hedgehog who's afraid of everything," said Belinda Blackbird.

"Why, he's so afraid that he stays rolled up like this all the time."

"That's not so bad," said Max. "That's what hedgehogs do."

"Hello, Henry," Molly said. "There are three of us here, and we've come from far away and would like to meet you."

He was very still for a moment, and then a tiny voice peeped, "Really?"

"We're going out into the world. Perhaps you two would like to come. Is there something special that you do well?" asked Max.

"I can't do anything," said Henry, sounding so sad. "I'm only good
  at being afraid."
"I hope you're not afraid of thunderstorms," said Molly.
"Oh, I am!" peeped Henry. "Why do you ask?"
"Well, my nose tells me there's one coming," said Molly.
"You're right. There'll be thunder and lightening soon," said Max as he
  noticed the big black clouds.

"Come on," said Belinda. "I know a place where we can hide from the storm."
Freddy, Max and Henry put Molly between them and all ran after Belinda.

Finally they stopped under some bushes.
Molly dug out a space in the ground.
"Oh no," cried Belinda. "It's starting to rain."
"Oh boy, ribbit, ribbit oh boy, fun in the rain,"
laughed Freddy.
He started jumping, and as he jumped he picked
a couple of big leaves to make a roof
for his friends.

"Hey, here's some soft hay," called Max as he once again
tripped over his own feet.
"Come on, Belinda, let's gather some
before it gets all wet."

Soon the five friends sat snugly in their little hiding place.
"I think we were great," said Molly. "One of us alone couldn't have
   done it."
"No, ribbit, ribbit ... never," said Freddy.
"You know," said Belinda, "it was easy because we each can do
   something well."
"Not me," said Henry. "I'm not good at thinking or smelling or jumping
   or flying... I'm only good at being afraid and being prickly."

"But you are great at being prickly!" said Max, "As a matter of fact,
when you're all rolled up with your spines sticking out,
you make a great prickly... ah... protector.
Would you be our prickly protector?"
"Oh yes!" said Henry, smiling for the first time.
"You know," said Max "It should always be like this,
where we can all help each other."

"Then we'll stay together," said the five friends. "We'll go out into the world and find our dreams and we'll stay all for one and one for all."